Windfall

Sara Cassidy

orca currents

ORCA BOOK PUBLISHERS

Library and Archives Canada Cataloguing in Publication

Cassidy, Sara
Windfall / Sara Cassidy.
(Orca currents)

Issued also in electronic formats.
ISBN 978-1-55469-850-9 (bound).--ISBN 978-1-55469-849-3 (pbk.)

I. Title. II. Series: Orca currents
PS8555.A7812W55 2011 JC813'.54 C2010-907992-2

First published in the United States, 2011
Library of Congress Control Number: 2010942077

Summary: Thirteen-year-old Liza, grieving the loss of a local homeless man and her family's apple tree, seeks healing through gardening.

Orca Book Publishers is dedicated to preserving the environment and has printed this book on paper certified by the Forest Stewardship Council.

Orca Book Publishers gratefully acknowledges the support for its publishing programs provided by the following agencies: the Government of Canada through the Canada Book Fund and the Canada Council for the Arts, and the Province of British Columbia through the BC Arts Council and the Book Publishing Tax Credit.

Cover design by Teresa Bubela
Cover photography by Dreamstime

ORCA BOOK PUBLISHERS
PO Box 5626, Stn. B
Victoria, BC Canada
V8R 6S4

ORCA BOOK PUBLISHERS
PO Box 468
Custer, WA USA
98240-0468

www.orcabook.com
Printed and bound in Canada.

14 13 12 11 • 4 3 2 1

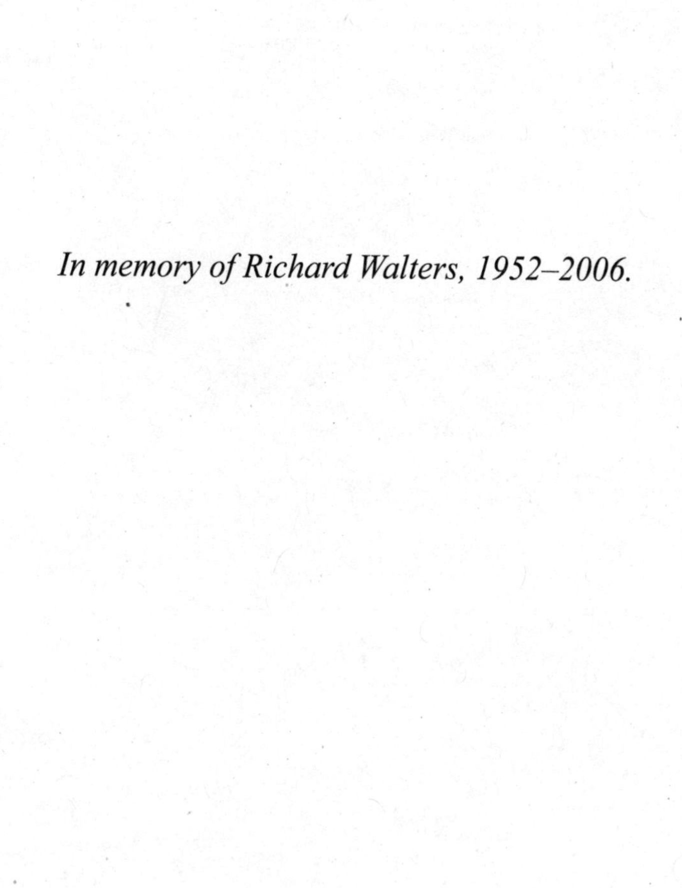

In memory of Richard Walters, 1952–2006.

Chapter One

Ri-i-i-ing. Ri-i-i-ing. Ri-i-i-ing. Ri-i-i-ing. I lift my head from my pillow. The downstairs floor squeaks. One of my brothers shuffles across their bedroom.

"Hullo?" It's Leland, who is six years old. After a long pause he says, "Do you want to speak to someone bigger?"

"I've got it, sweetheart." Mom picks up the phone in her room. She speaks quietly for a few minutes.

"Kids!" she calls. "I need to talk to you."

The three of us bound to her room. The boys are wearing flannel pajamas with pictures of robots and snowboarders. Their hair is stormy with sleep. Silas has eight little circles indented on his cheek. It looks like he slept on a piece of Lego. I'm wearing the knee-length soccer shirt that Dad sent from England.

Mom smiles at us, but when she blinks, tears slide from her eyes.

"Sad news," she says. "Richard died last night."

"Outside?" Silas asks, horrified.

"Yes, dear," Mom says. "In the park."

"Alone?" Leland asks in a wobbly voice.

"I guess so," Mom says gently.

"Richard slept outside and alone for many years."

"Was it rainy and cold?" Leland's chin trembles.

"It was a lovely night," Mom says. She shoots me a look. Mom and I played Crazy Eights last night after the boys went to sleep. Rain pelted the roof, and the wind was so strong that the branches of the backyard apple tree scratched at the window.

Still, maybe Richard was warm and dry. Maybe in his dreams angels rocked him into that weird final sleep. You never know.

"He was probably dreaming beautiful dreams," I say to comfort Leland.

"Probably?" Leland challenges.

"Maybe probably," I say.

"Maybe *maybe*," Leland says.

"We brought him a coat not that long ago," Silas says. "And socks. He would have been warm."

"We gave him money every time we saw him," Mom says airily. She looks out the window at another gray Victoria day.

She's right, we did. But we never invited him for supper, or for a shower, or a night in a warm bed. We have an unused bedroom in the basement he could have lived in.

"We won't ever, ever see him again, right?" Leland asks.

"That's right, except in your memories." Mom starts making her bed. "There will be a funeral in a few days."

Leland goes rigid. He clenches his teeth. "I'm not going to a funeral!" he says, staring Mom down.

"Me neither," Silas mutters, his eyes on the floor.

"Liza?" Mom looks surprised. "Surely, you'll go?"

"No way," I declare. I picture Richard, wax-white and unmoving on his bench.

I imagine rain on his lifeless face. What was I thinking—*angels*? *Warmth*? He was just as alone when he died as he was in life.

Mom sits again on her bed and studies our faces. She opens her arms to Leland. He resists at first, but then melts into her lap.

"Look, you guys," Mom whispers. "This is sad. Even a little frightening. We didn't know Richard well, but we loved him. He was sweet. Gentle."

"Yeah," Leland sniffles, raising his head from Mom's shoulder. "His gentleness was more important than his smelliness."

Silas and I both snort. We try to stifle our laughter.

"Maybe you'll change your minds," Mom continues, ignoring us. "A funeral is a chance to say goodbye." She grins, then singsongs, "You'd miss a bit of school."

A bribe? How can she be so cold? Richard is *dead*, and we're supposed to get excited about missing school?

"Yeah, that'll make it worth it," I say bitterly as I leave the room.

"Liza, I didn't mean it that way. I'm sorry. We're all upset," Mom calls after me.

At breakfast my food tastes so dry, it hurts my throat. My orange juice stings. The yellow kitchen walls, normally cheerful, are dull. It's like the light's been sucked out of the house.

Neighbors keep calling. The phone sounds robotic and shrill. I hear Mom refer to Richard as being "gone" or "passed on." Once, she says he's "crossed over." Crossed over to where? Some sunshiny happy place? I've seen police shows. I know Richard is in a steel drawer in a frosty room with a numbered tag around his big toe.

Between phone calls, Mom makes the boys' lunches. She spreads peanut butter on slices of bread and fills Tupperware with grapes and animal crackers as if it's just another day. The boys hunker over their Lego as if nothing remarkable has happened. Nobody cares that an entire person has gone—*poof!*—out like a light. Shouldn't we all be bawling? Shouldn't the world stop spinning for a moment?

Or maybe it doesn't matter that Richard is dead. Did it matter that he was alive? All he did was sit on a bench and sleep in the bushes of Meegan Park. We passed him nearly every day on our way to school or to the store. He never held out his hand, but Mom always gave him a fistful of change. She always asked how he was. Richard always replied in his warm thick voice, "Good."

Was he good? He was dirty! His hair was a pile of knots, and his clothes were stained and torn. He was always bundled in layers of coats, pants, shirts and sweaters. He even wore wool hats in the middle of summer. You'd know him from a block away. He was rumpled and baggy, like a hulking pile of laundry.

"Check it out!" Silas shouts as we enter Meegan Park on our way to school. He's pointing at Richard's bench. Someone has laid a huge sunflower and a framed photograph of Richard there. In the photograph, Richard is sitting on the very same bench. His warm bristly face looks calmly at the camera. A hand-printed note is propped against the sunflower's thick stem. It says *Rest in Peace, Richard.*

Leland swings his backpack to the ground and pulls out his lunch kit. He takes an apple and places it on the bench between the jar and the picture.

"There," he says, his chin wobbling.

The apple gleams in the morning sun. It seems to swell against its taut red skin, bursting with life. We continue on to school. We'll be late now. Maybe the world did stop spinning for an instant. As I turn away from Richard's bench, the nearby bushes rustle. A few fall leaves scatter to the ground. I get a strong feeling that Richard is watching us. It's spooky, but it's not scary.

Chapter Two

<<Come in, Olive. Come in. Over.>>

<< Hi, Liza! Over.>>

<<What are you doing? Over.>>

<<Mending socks. And digesting lentil soup. Over.>>

<<Tree house? Over.>>

<<Tree house. Over.>>

<<Go-t—ing—O-er.>>

<<You're breaking up. Tree house. Over.>>

I got walkie-talkies last month for my birthday. I wanted a cell phone, but Mom is too cheap. Well, that's not how *she* tells it.

"Cell phones mess with your brain," she says. "Radio waves equal radiation. Radiation spells tumors. Experts predict a brain-cancer tsunami in ten years. No one under eighteen should use cell phones—except in an emergency."

Olive is my neighbor and best friend. It's a cool September evening, so I throw a jean jacket over my sweater as I head out to the tree house. These are the best weeks of the year, because I can reach out the tree-house window and pick apples straight from the branch. I'm munching one when Olive straggles up.

"Bad news," Olive puffs. "I looked everywhere for batteries. We're out." She gives me a look. What she's really saying is that our walkie-talkie days are over.

"I can get some," I say.

"No," Olive says gravely. "That would be cheating."

Three months ago, Olive's family decided not to buy anything new *for a year*. Except food. I started it. I'd learned that an oil company was polluting farmland in Guatemala and not compensating local farmers. I formed Girls for Renewable Resources, Really! We protested and got the company to pay up.

Olive joined GRRR!, but her parents didn't want Olive getting too involved. When she couldn't come to our protest, Olive got her parents to watch *An Inconvenient Truth*, a movie about global warming. They were so freaked out about carbon levels that they decided Olive *had* to be in GRRR! They vowed to reuse, reduce and recycle with a vengeance.

So, if Olive is out of batteries, our walkie-talkie days are over.

"Morse code?" I propose. "Telegraph?"

Olive giggles. "How about semaphore flags?"

"Carrier pigeon!" I say. "Smoke signals."

"We could just yell," Olive points out. "It isn't *that* far."

"We *could* put a string between our houses, and zip-line notes to each other." I'm serious this time.

"A laundry line would do the trick," Olive muses.

"No." I grin. "I've got an idea. Let me surprise you."

"Okay." Liza plucks an apple from a branch and takes a noisy bite. She frowns. "Sad news about Richard, huh?"

"Yeah," I say. "It's weird. He just sat there and never talked. You would think you wouldn't miss him. But it feels so big, so *loud*, that he's gone."

Olive nods. "I know. Mom says he made us anxious in a good way. He reminded us how lucky we are to have a warm home."

"Maybe," I say. "I just wanted *him* to be warm, in a little apartment somewhere, and not always on public display."

"Well, he's not on public display now," Olive deadpans.

"That's for sure," I say. "He has vanished. Disappeared."

I remember the feeling I had in the park. "Where *do* you think he is?" I ask.

"Nowhere," Olive says. "We're just a mass of electrical impulses, Liza. Without our bodies, we're like a DVD without a DVD player. There's no picture, no sound, no story. The only life after death is the worms that feast on your body and the plants that shoot up as you rot away."

"Ugh, Olive! Fat worms and a crop of tulips? *That's* life after death?"

"What do *you* think? That Richard's an angel, floating around looking down on us? Or that he's"—she puts on a spooky voice—"a ghost?"

I try to think up an answer. Then the tree house groans. It sways, and then boards tear from each other with a screech, leaving raw edges and bent nails waving in the air.

Olive and I freeze. We stare wildly into each other's eyes. We're half smirking, as if it's funny, and half terrified. Suddenly, the entire tree house skids down the tree trunk, scraping off bark and snapping branches. I protect my eyes with one hand and grab the windowsill with the other. Olive screams.

Then—*whomp*—it stops. My tailbone throbs. Olive moans and rubs the back of her head. We sit for a few moments.

Then, slowly and without a word, we ease ourselves out the little doorway and leap to the ground. We run like mad, yelping and laughing. We fall onto the lawn, clutching each other.

Chapter Three

There's a wide circle of yellow caution tape around the apple tree. Actually, it's a yellow streamer. My enviro-mom doesn't like plastic, but she didn't want to pay for biodegradable caution tape. You have to buy it in bulk. "Let's hope we *never* need five hundred feet of caution tape," Mom told the hardware store clerk.

Silas made a sign: *Tree Ailing: Do Not Climb*. The entire tree is on a slant.

"Like the leaning tower of Pisa," Silas comments at breakfast.

"Tilting," Mom says, launching our family game.

"Listing," I say.

"Lurching," Silas says.

"Diagonal?" Leland says.

"Sloping," Mom says.

"Off balance," I say.

"*I'm* off balance." Leland pouts as he sadly stirs his cereal.

I am too. Our apple tree was the first tree we climbed. Every fall, the kitchen shelves fill with jars of applesauce. If our generous tree is going to tilt, then our lives will too.

"Our tree has had a long life," Mom says. "It's been growing for over a hundred years, long before this house was built. I asked John Allans."

"The dude with the top hat who gives ghost tours?" I ask.

"That *dude*," Mom chides with a smile, "is a local historian. He says our apple tree was part of a huge orchard. This land was once all farmers' fields. I've called an arborist to come over and give a diagnosis. And when I'm in Duncan next week, I'm taking some of our apples to a pomologist."

Mom's going to Duncan to help the museum put a dollar value on their collection. There's a pile of butter churns, chamber pots, saddles, even tractors from a farm that is being razed to make room for apartment buildings. Mom is an art historian. She helps museums and auction houses figure out what they've got and what it's worth.

"How's a palm reader going to help?" Silas asks.

"Pomologist. Think *pomme*. French for apple," Mom says. "A pomologist studies fruit. She's going to tell us what kind of apples we've been eating all these years. The arborist—her name is Imogen—is a tree doctor."

"She'll say it has to be cut down," Silas says gloomily.

"Yes, she might," Mom agrees.

"That would leave a big empty space," Leland grouses. He is stirring his cereal into sodden mush.

"Yeah," I say. I feel close to tears. "You might as well yank my heart out."

"Hey!" Leland cries. "An apple is probably the same size as your heart. It's even shaped like a heart." Then he goes quiet. We all do. None of us finish breakfast.

Chapter Four

<<Can you hear me? Over.>>

<<Awesome! Over.>>

<<Cool! I hear you too! Over.>>

<<The arborist just got here. Over.>>

<<I'll be right there. Over and out.>>

The "lovers' phone" works! I made it with two tin cans and some fishing line. Now, that's technology! I hammered a hole through the bottom of each can, poked the line through and knotted it. If we hold the line taut and it doesn't touch anything, the vibrations of our voices travel down the string. They enter the can on the other end and swirl into our ears. When I want to talk, I just yank on the string. Olive hears her end clang against her windowsill and "answers" her tin.

Making stuff helps me relax. I mend the broken, rescue the forgotten and invent what's needed. I've turned T-shirts into pillows, stitched juice Tetra Paks into wallets, and made a self-watering plant pot from a pop bottle. It's called DIY—Do It Yourself.

Imogen, the arborist, leaps down from her battered pickup truck. She is wearing faded jeans and work boots. I guess she's in her twenties. Her long reddish hair looks alive. Her T-shirt proclaims *God is just an abbreviation for Goddess*.

Imogen goes straight to our tree and climbs it with ease. Olive, the boys and I perch along the top of the fence and watch her poke at the bark and cut off a few twigs.

"You guys are sure glum," she says after a while.

"I've been climbing that tree since before I could walk," Silas says. "I even talk to it."

"Me too," Leland admits. "I lie on the ground and look up through its branches at the sky."

"Trees make great friends," Imogen says. "They're wise."

"They're not just quiet," Leland says. "They know *how* to be quiet."

"Yeah." Imogen stops for a moment. "Imagine how loud the world would be if there were no trees."

"Mom says it was part of an orchard, like, a century ago," I say.

"That's for sure," Imogen says. "If you climb high up and look into your neighbors' yards, you'll see other trees from the orchard."

"Can we really still climb it?" Silas asks.

"Just don't go under the tree house. And avoid this area." Imogen points to a split in the trunk. "You should be all right if you climb that side. But your tree is likely infected with Armillaria, or honey fungus. It's a root disease that spreads to other trees. I'm sorry, kids, but it looks as though your friend will have to come down."

My throat burns. Silas looks to the sky, trying to keep his tears from falling. They trickle toward his ears. Olive knits her eyebrows as if she can think herself out of this situation. And Leland? He slides down from the fence and stretches his arms around our tree's rough trunk. "It's okay," we hear him whisper. "It will be all right."

After Imogen leaves, Olive and I step branch to branch, climbing up, up, up. When we get as high as we can, we look across the neighborhood.

"There!" Olive cries out, pointing. Sure enough, there's an apple tree in the backyard of the house two doors down. "There too!" she says excitedly. We see tree after tree. The neighborhood unfolds before us. The trees may be separated by fences, but they're in a pattern.

"Wow," Olive breathes. "We live in an orchard!"

It is amazing. All these years, these trees have been quietly growing apples and sleeping through winter. They are uncomplaining and patient—like Richard.

Chapter Five

Richard's funeral is today. Halfway through the morning, Mrs. Reynolds pages Silas, Leland and me to her office. Mrs. Reynolds is our new principal. She loves rules. Some of the kids call her Mrs. Killjoy. It's mean. She makes us feel mean. Our school was a happy place before she arrived. Since she took over, we're no longer allowed to use teachers' first names or make calls on the office phone unless it's a matter of life or death. We're not allowed to throw balls against the school wall or climb in the ravine behind the school.

When Mrs. Reynolds started as principal, she met with about forty students. She met with Abelius, who has impulse-control issues; in kindergarten, he squished a caterpillar we were all sketching. Another kid she called in was Janine, who's in my grade and still isn't reading. She met with this kid Max, who is super artistic but cries a lot, and Amelia, who is really, really large.

She called in all the kids who sort of stuck out, or weren't normal, whatever that means. That included me, Leland and Silas. She mentioned that we were late for school often and said something about how difficult life must be for our single mom.

"It's not difficult, it's fun," Leland said.

"It must be hard not having a dad," Mrs. Reynolds said.

"We *have* a dad," I said, surprised by the anger in my voice. "He just lives far away."

"I see," she said snidely, as if our dad didn't want to see us, which is total bunk.

"We're usually late because I'm building with Lego and Leland is coloring and Liza is playing chess with Mom," explained Silas. "We're late because we're happy."

Mrs. Reynolds's mouth opened and shut and opened again. She looked like a trout.

"Mom works hard," Leland said thoughtfully. "All single moms do."

Silas and I tried not to laugh.

Leland looked at us. "Well, that's what Mom says!"

Silas and I shook with laughter. Leland laughed too. Mrs. Reynolds stood up to let us know we could go.

So now we're in her office again. It's totally tidy. The pencils in the pencil jar are all nibs up and perfectly sharpened. The three books on her shelf are about business management. The one plant is plastic. Nothing is out of place. Mom once said that Mrs. Reynolds was a "control freak."

Mrs. Reynolds takes a stuffed owl down from a shelf and drops it into Leland's lap. I guess it's supposed to make him feel comfortable. "Your mom called to say she is taking you out of school before recess. Where are you going?"

My mouth locks. It's none of her business where we're going. Silas gazes out the window.

"To a funeral," Leland answers.

"Oh. I'm sorry to hear that," Mrs. Reynolds says with genuine sympathy—I think.

"Yeah, it's not a *fun*-eral." Leland snickers at his own joke. "Mom says Silas and I can stay in the car, but Liza's going into the graveyard."

"Who died?" Mrs. Reynolds asks.

I close my eyes and frown. I'm trying to keep her out. Leland's too young to realize she's being nosy.

"A friend," Leland says. "Well, a neighbor, kind of. But not the kind that has a house. He slept in the park."

"Oh?" Mrs. Reynolds's head jerks back. "A homeless person?"

"Kind of." Leland glances at Silas. Tears run down Silas's cheeks as he looks out the window.

"His name was Richard," I burst out.

I stand to leave and motion to my brothers to follow. I want to get out of there. Only Leland says goodbye. Mrs. Reynolds says nothing.

We sit on the edge of a planter in the schoolyard and have our snacks. Mom drives up as I finish my carrot. There is no garbage can, so I ram the end of my carrot into the planter's soil. I leave the green end sticking out. "Liza!" Silas hisses. Then he shoves his carrot into the dirt too.

On the way to the Royal Oak Burial Park, I breathe on the car window and write my name in the mist. The end of my finger is dirty from the planter. I think of Mrs. Reynolds with her tidy office and her clean hands. Richard was dirty and rumpled and didn't have a job or money, but he was a better person than Mrs. Reynolds.

Chapter Six

The boys and I like the idea of missing school, but none of us wants to stand by Richard's grave. I'm wearing a skirt and itchy tights. At least Mom agreed I could wear high-tops and a jean jacket, seeing as Richard wasn't exactly Mr. Fancy.

Mom thought it was better for the boys to sit in the parking lot than not to go at all. "It's different from normal to be in a hot car in the middle of nowhere. Doing things differently is a way to honor death," she explains as we drive along. "Death makes things strange. It makes us look at everything again. In a way, it wakes things up."

"Like that tree over Richard's bench," Silas leaps in. "I never noticed it before. But now that there's no Richard, it's like it sings. It's a really neat tree. It's got long droopy branches like a willow, except it can't be a willow—the leaves are shaped like keyholes."

"A weeping oak," Mom murmurs.

"The bench sure stands out now," Leland adds. "It's so empty, it shines."

"I feel guilty when I see it," Silas says. "Like I'm betraying him."

"Survivors' guilt," Mom says. "You feel guilty that you're alive and he isn't."

"Yeah," Silas says. "And I felt guilty when he was alive because I had a house and nice clothes."

"Why *didn't* he have anything?" Leland asks. "Why did he live outside?"

"I don't really know," Mom says. "But he probably had a mental illness."

"He was sick in his mind?" Silas asks.

"More like his mind didn't help him get the things he needed," Mom says. She pulls the car into a parking lot that's empty except for two other cars. "Here we are."

The boys pull out their books. Mom insisted they pack serious books, no comics. That was more respectful. She and I stroll across the huge lawn of the "park." It is surprisingly beautiful, quiet and treed. We're careful not to step on the plaques in the grass that mark where people's ashes are buried. Their tidy rows remind me of the orchard.

At a knee-high pile of dirt, we meet up with our neighbor, Nicole, and two men who introduce themselves as Richard's neighbors. I ask if they left the sunflower and the photograph, and they nod. Nicole has learned that Richard had no living relatives, so the city is paying for his cremation.

"I'll bet Richard would have preferred a green burial," Nicole says. She tells us about her mother's "green" funeral in England. In a green burial, she says, the body is put in a biodegradable casket, something like cardboard or bamboo. The body isn't preserved with formaldehyde to make it last. "You *want* the body to rot. Or, sorry, to decompose," she says. "Family and friends plant native plants on the burial mound. There are no stone slabs or bronze plaques. Instead, the grave becomes part of the ecosystem."

A tall bony man in dark jeans and a loose suit jacket strides toward us. He carries a simple wood box. Mom puts her arm around me as I realize with a shock that Richard is in the box. Well, his ashes are.

The thin man introduces himself as Mitchell Harlan. He's a church minister who tries to help people living on the street. He often visited Richard.

"We are here to remember and say farewell to Richard Karl Lind," he begins. It's a shock to hear Richard's full name. "Richard was a gentle, very private person who lived in public. He was a man of few words, but he did once tell me that his parents died in a car accident. He was left alone in the world at nineteen years old. Perhaps he never recovered. He lived in Meegan Park for twenty-seven years, often inviting the kindness of strangers—"

"And neighbors," Nicole breaks in.

"Yes," Mitchell agrees. "Richard had a gift for turning strangers into neighbors. And you did your best to make him *your* neighbor.

"Richard accepted his fate, though I believe he accepted it too well. I never learned to what extent Richard chose the life he lived. In my mind, he was a mild and meek soul who didn't know how to ask for help.

"Only two weeks ago, I said to him, 'Richard, you are getting too old to be sleeping outside.' 'I know,' he agreed. I said, 'How about we finally get you a bed somewhere?' 'Okay,' he said." Mitchell imitates Richard's thick voice, and we smile. "It was the first time he had ever agreed—" Tears stream from Mitchell's eyes. A crow flies overhead, so close we hear its wings beat against the air. "Well, Richard," he continues. "This sure isn't the home I imagined for you. But I am glad you are here, in the splendor of this old park. I hope you will be at home in this place."

Mitchell invites us each to say a few words. Nicole speaks first. "Richard, you always reminded me to take in the world around me, to question my hurry and my greed. You made me thankful for what I have," she says. "Goodbye."

Mom reads a poem called "This is what was bequeathed us." She tells us it is by Gregory Orr, an American poet. It's about what people are left with when someone dies. The last part goes:

No other shore, only this bank
On which the living gather.

No meaning but what we find here.
No purpose but what we make.

That, and the beloved's clear
instructions:
Turn me into song; sing me awake.

The two men say in unison, "Peace be with you, Richard."

Then it's my turn. My mouth is dry. I feel weird. I've never said anything more to Richard than "Hi." Now, words work slowly from my mouth, difficult as gravel, "Thank you, Richard."

Mitchell lowers the small box into the hole in the ground, fills the hole with dirt and lays a plaque with Richard's name on top.

In the morning, I had picked a few late-blooming flowers from the park, even though Silas reminded me we weren't allowed to. The park is a protected area. I decided an exception could be made for Richard. He had lived in the park for so long. I lay my bouquet beside the plaque.

"Beautiful," Nicole whispers.

I feel like a hypocrite. Why didn't I give Richard flowers when he was alive? Was I afraid of him? Is it easier to be kind to him now that he's dead?

Mom tucks a few toonies into the fresh dirt of the grave, and everyone stands there.

After a few minutes, the adults start chatting about the weather, the traffic and a new highway overpass. I can't believe it! How can they talk about such stupid things? Then they're joking with each other, waving goodbye with a cheery "great to see you."

I look back at the place where the trees bow over Richard's remains, as if they know he is there. I remember how I said "thank you." What was I thanking him for?

For not getting angry that I did nothing to help him?

"You look mad, Liza," Silas says when I get back to the car. I *am* angry at the stupid adults with their meaningless prattle. But something else is bothering me. I'm angry at Richard! For what? For making me feel helpless for so long?

I picture him in his dirty clothes, with his knotted hair, and I feel annoyed. I am tired of feeling bad for him. It isn't my fault he was the way he was. I dive into one of the books the boys packed. By the time we are back at school, I have forgotten about Richard.

Chapter Seven

I’m putting the nose on a papier-mâché piggy bank for Leland when the lovers’ phone rattles with force. Silas holds the tin can to my ear, since my hands are covered with goo.

<<I’ve had it! Over.>>

<<Had what? Over.>>

<<I want to take a shower. A *real* shower. Over.>>

<<Come here then! Over and out.>>

A moment later, Olive bursts into our kitchen. "That's it! I want a shower with real soap and real shampoo. I've been washing my hair with eggs and beer for seven months. I want new clothes. And a new book—smelly-new, you know? I want the cover to crackle when I open it, like there's a secret between me and the book. I know a secondhand book tells the same story, but I want something that's *all* mine. I want socks that fit like they were made for *my* feet. I *know* tons of fossil fuels are burned to make them and package them and ship them from China. Oh yeah, I know it."

"Socks from China?" Leland is amazed. "That's over the sea, right?"

"Olive, you're normally so unflappable," Mom says. "Imperturbable."

"Unrufflable," Silas adds.

"Unshakeable," I put in.

"Dispassionate."

"Nonchalant."

"Downright unflusterable."

"Not anymore!" Olive fires back. "I'm perturbed. Ruffled. Flustered. Flapped!" She cracks a smile. "Seriously, Mom won't even get me new *shoes*!"

We all look down. Her runners look like they've been clawed by raccoons.

"Hey," Mom says gently. "Liza has some old—barely worn—shoes that might fit you. Hop in the shower. I'll see what I can find."

Olive looks sheepish. "You know, I love living simply. Really. I like biking everywhere. We have more time together as a family since we're not running around shopping for this and that. I've learned to mend and be resourceful and self-reliant. I've tried to be happy with what I've got."

"You want a little buffing up," Mom suggests.

"Something in the latest style?" I venture.

"No!" Olive says. "I look at the girls at school dressed in the latest from the Gap, and I can see they're naked underneath. I'm not a pervert—I mean I see who they *are*. *Here*. *Now.* Maybe you have to live the way I've been living to understand that."

"I think I understand it," Silas says. I'm not surprised. Silas is happy being his dreamy self, and he's no flashy dresser.

"I'm tired of everything I have," Olive continues. "And I've read everything in the library."

"Here." Mom hands Olive a fluffy pile of bath towel, face towel and facecloth. She plunks a bar of soap still in its wrapper and an unopened bottle of shampoo from her last hotel stay on top. "The spa awaits."

While Olive is in the shower, Mom, Silas, Leland and I ransack our closets and bookshelves and fill a basket with clothes and a box with books. I can't believe how much stuff we have that we don't need.

Olive tears up when she sees them. "Thanks," she says. "I feel better. Ready for Round Two of walking with a small footprint."

She leaves our house scrubbed and shining and dressed head-to-toe in "new" clothes.

The phone rings. Mom answers. "Shhh!" she says to us. "It's the pomologist." Into the phone Mom says, "Oh, I see...uh-huh...Isn't that amazing!... No kidding...Wow, really? That's unbelievable...Right, no problem... Got it...yes. Thank you," and hangs up.

"It's a Winter Rambo!" she tells us. "Pale yellow skin streaked red, tender sub-acid flesh. Asymmetrical in shape. Sweet flavor. It's been in the records—in England and the United States—for six hundred years! Shakespeare could have eaten one!"

It's cool to know the name of our beloved apple. Now, the tree has a history. It gives me the same feeling as when I heard Richard's full name at the funeral. I feel like I can do something about the tree, save it maybe. As for Richard Karl Lind, maybe I could do something for him too.

At supper, Mom says that loading Olive up with all our extra stuff reminded her of a job she once did. She was helping Kwakwaka'wakw people insure potlatch objects that a museum was returning to them. The museum was repatriating these items a hundred years after basically stealing them from the First Nation community. Mom explains that the word *potlatch* means "to give away" or "a gift." A potlatch is a party thrown by the hereditary chief or a wealthy family in the community. The main purpose is to share wealth, which includes stories and songs.

"In the past they shared dried food, fish oil, even canoes," Mom explains. "A family's status was raised not by having a lot, but by how they shared." She gets a book from the shelf and opens it to a photo of an awesome-looking man with dark hair and a strong nose. "This is Chief O'waxalagalis of the Kwakwaka'wakw. He said, 'It is a strict law that bids us distribute our property among our friends and neighbors. It is a good law.' But the Europeans outlawed the potlatch. They considered it uncivilized!"

"Uncivilized to share stuff?" Silas asks. "That's crazy!"

"It threatened the European view of economics—you can't just *give* stuff away!" Mom says. "The Europeans raided potlatches and arrested people. They seized ceremonial objects and gifts. They took food, ornately carved masks, feast bowls, you name it. First Nations are still asking for these items back. Once in a while, a museum does the right thing."

I leaf through the book and come across a photograph of three people dressed in woven capes. They are wearing shining earrings made, the book says, from abalone shells. They stand in front of a huge wooden building.

"That's a longhouse," Mom tells me. "Several families lived together in one building. They were very common along our coast."

"How big were they?"

"Well, it says this one was fifty feet by a hundred feet. So, five thousand square feet," Mom says. "Probably seven or eight families lived in it. That's the size of that house going up on Dallas Road. That house is for only one family. Four people."

"How big is *our* house?" I ask.

"Twelve hundred square feet," Mom answers.

"And that's big enough? I mean, are we happy?" The question leaps from my mouth.

"We're very close," Mom says, reaching out and ruffling my hair.

It's true. We're usually at each other's elbows. "We keep each other warm," I say, without really thinking.

"There's truth to that, Liza." Mom nods. "I'm always amazed how little oil we need to heat this house."

Chapter Eight

Olive and I are out riding our bikes on the weekend when I recognize a tall man carrying a box to the curb. It's Mitchell Harlan, the minister from Richard's funeral. "Hi!" I call. "Remember me?"

Mitchell tilts his head one way, then another. He squints, and then his face relaxes. "Of course! The memorial!

Funny. I was just thinking of Richard. I always do when I put out a box."

We look down at a cardboard carton filled with red apples. "This is the fourth I've lugged across the yard this fall. My apple tree is going bananas. Or it's going apples. A bumper crop."

Mitchell invites us in for tea and apple cake. I explain that Olive knew Richard too.

"I always felt comfortable with Richard," Mitchell says, slicing the cake. "With some people who live on the street, I'm on my guard. They've had difficult lives and are often angry for good reason. But even though they have good reason to be angry, that doesn't mean they won't bite. You have to be careful. Richard wasn't at all like that."

"He was sweet," Olive says.

Mitchell looks at us carefully. He bites his lip. "I'm going to tell you something," he finally says. "It's a sad story, but it teaches. All Richard ever asked me for was fresh fruit and vegetables. I liked how he said vegetables. He said every syllable—*ve-ge-ta-bles*. When you're eating from food banks, you get a lot of donuts and bread and canned food. Nothing fresh.

"One afternoon I got a call from the police. Richard had gone into someone's yard and taken a few apples. The people who lived there were not happy. To them, he was just some dirty intruder." Mitchell shakes his head. "Poor Richard."

"What happened?" Olive and I chorus. We're horrified.

"If you were the police, what would you do? The officers led Richard out of the yard, but there was no way they were going to arrest him. They could have charged him with trespass and theft. The homeowners wanted them to.

The police asked me to talk to them. I sat at their kitchen table, and I told them Richard was harmless. I told them he had gotten confused. I said he would never trespass again. That's what they wanted to hear.

"It was weeks before Richard stopped trembling. I did my best to comfort him, but he didn't sleep well for many nights."

Mitchell reached for the teapot and topped up our cups. "The saddest thing was that Richard didn't even pick those apples," he said. "He just gathered windfall."

"Windfall?" I asked.

"Apples that fall to the ground because of wind or the simple pull of gravity."

Mitchell looked at us sadly. "When I was a boy, my mom would ask me, 'If a hungry man steals a loaf of bread, is it really stealing?' I believe food can't be stolen. Hunger is different from greed."

Olive nods. "My mom says that if someone asks for water, we should always say yes. And if we're sharing a cup of water with someone, it's wrong to drink more than our share. Water belongs equally to everyone."

"I hate those companies that put it in bottles and sell it," I say sourly.

"Some say that water, air *and* land belong to everyone equally. They say that property is theft—just by owning something, you've taken it. I agree," Mitchell says. "I certainly believe that my apples are common property. Especially after what happened to Richard. That's why I put them out for neighbors."

Olive and I pedal home with plastic bags of Mitchell's apples hanging from our handlebars. At one point I tease Olive about having an emotion to report.

At Olive's house before supper, everyone holds hands and talks about how they felt that day.

"That story sure was sad," Olive says. "Imagine calling the police for something like that."

I'm not feeling sad though. I'm actually feeling kind of happy. I'm happy Richard *did* something. He tried to get what he needed.

It's funny how I keep being reminded of Richard. Mitchell's story and the bag of apples bumping against my knee as I pedal keep Richard close. Even the startling emptiness of Richard's bench is an echo of his life. But echoes eventually die too, don't they?

Chapter Nine

At lunch, someone grabs my elbow. It's Niall. As far as I'm concerned, he is the cutest boy in the school. His wavy black hair shines down past his shoulders. He's the school high-jump champion, wiry and nimble. He has a perpetual cold, which means there's not a lot of competition for dating him. Niall makes supercool stuff. He once connected an amplifier to the cutlery drawer so the rattling of knives and forks was broadcast through his house. He did the same thing with a drainpipe. He called it audio art. Usually Niall is mellow, but today he seems agitated.

"Liza, I'm going to propose a compost program," he says. Niall is in BRRR!, Boys for Renewable Resources, Really! They're GRRR!'s sibling organization. "It's cheap and simple. A bucket in every classroom for lunch scraps. We only need to find a farmer to pick up the compost once a week."

"I can find a farmer," I say, a little too eagerly. Mom knows a few farmers.

"Killjoy will probably say no," says Niall, "unless there's a whole lot of support for it."

Mrs. Reynolds—Killjoy—has blocked every one of BRRR!'s and GRRR!'s initiatives. Last year we held a bicycle wash and a plant sale. We raised hundreds of dollars for solar hot-water panels for the school. But Mrs. Reynolds said the panels were aesthetically detrimental. She meant they were ugly.

"I was going to ask if you would help me draw up a petition and collect signatures," says Niall.

A petition sounds exciting—if I'm working on it with *him*.

Niall and I spend the rest of the lunch hour in the library. We laugh a lot trying to get the wording right. The petition can't be too brazen or too shy.

Niall asks where I had gone last week. He'd seen me and the boys get in Mom's car. I tell him a little about Richard.

"Yeah, I used to see him around," Niall says. "He was just a bum."

"Well, I don't know," I say, surprised Niall would be so cold. "He was homeless."

"Yeah, I know. Lots of those guys on the street are totally fine, and young. Why don't they just get a job?"

"Well, he was sick, I think. He lost his parents when he was young, and never recovered."

"Come on, Liza. Isn't that lame?" Niall said. "I mean, if my parents died, I'd be freaked, but I'd recover. Why are we supposed to feel sorry for these people? They don't do anything to help themselves."

For a second, I want to agree with Niall. If it was Richard's fault that he was the way he was, I wouldn't have to feel bad about the way he died.

But I surprise myself. I say something I'd never thought through before: "Maybe that *was* the best Richard could do."

Niall considers this. "Okay. Maybe," he says. "But, come on. How could he live like that?"

"I wonder about that too," I say. "But I don't know what went on in his head.

Maybe he was thinking about cool things, having beautiful daydreams. He was serene."

"Passive."

"So what? Do we always have to be doing, making, taking, shopping?" I ask. "Look at my friend, Olive. Her family decided not to buy anything for a whole year."

"That's crazy!"

"It's good for the environment. And they say it's kind of spiritual. There was a lot of stuff they thought they needed, but really, they only wanted it."

"But that's not as humiliating as living on the street," Niall says. "Besides, there's nothing wrong with *wanting* something, Liza. Needs are basic: food, shelter. But what's life without friendship"—he looks at me—"or, say, art?"

"Richard walked with a really light footprint," I point out.

"That wasn't what he was trying to do. He suffered too much," Niall says. "He was bent over, wrinkled up and worn out. He was not thriving. And what did he give anyone else? Nothing!"

"Well, he wasn't *hurting* anyone," I sputter. "People say that he made them slow down and count their blessings."

"He didn't mean to. Those were accidental benefits," Niall says. "He was lazy."

"He was supremely gentle," I say.

"Stupefied."

"He wasn't totally healthy," I say. "Or he was shut out. There was nothing for him to do."

"I guess," Niall considers.

"Richard may not have intended to make a difference by living the way he did, but the fact is, he did make a difference," I say. "He certainly never meant harm. Which is a lot more than you can say for others—like oil companies."

Niall smiles. "I never thought it through before. You're smart, Liza."

I feel warm. Then I feel too warm. My heart pounds and my face burns, and possibly my hair stands on end.

"You too," I mumble.

Luckily, Niall shifts gears. "Let's print these off." We argue over the best font and then send the petition to the printer.

A couple of days later, Niall and I meet in the library to tally up our signatures. Between the two of us, we have collected 246 names. Some of the kindergartners signed in crayon.

"That's ninety-two percent of the student body," Niall gloats as we staple the pages together.

"I'd photocopy those if I were you," says Mme. Falette, our school librarian. She gives us a knowing look and says something about despots and destruction of records.

Ten minutes later, we slide the thick petition into Mrs. Reynolds's mailbox.

"She can't possibly say no," Niall says, turning to me. "What do you think?"

I'd been thinking that I had to get a little braver on the girl-likes-boy-who-maybe-likes-girl-back front. "I think we make a good team," I say, putting out my fist. He taps it with his.

"I'm down with that," he says and grins.

I feel my hair rise again. When Niall looks back as he hops on his bike, he probably thinks I've been electrocuted.

From: LittleLizaJane@whoohoo.com

To: listserve, GRRR!

Subject: Don't tell Olive!

Hi Everyone!

I'm hosting a surprise clothing and book exchange in honor of Olive's family's crazy/amazing year-long commitment to live with what they have.

Come to my house on Saturday at 1:00 PM with books you've already read and clothes you're tired of.

We'll spread everything out. Everyone gets a number, and we take turns choosing two items from the pile. We keep going until no one wants anything.

I'll make sure there's a change room, mirrors and snacks.

We'll probably have clothes and books left over. Could someone volunteer to take them to the Women in Need thrift shop after the party?

Hope to see you there! Don't tell Olive!

Liza

Chapter Ten

Leland is howling. Silas is perched on a branch, bawling. Imogen stands between them, looking helpless in spite of the chain saw in her hands. Today, her T-shirt says *Weeds are flowers too. —Eeyore*.

"Hey, Leland," Mom soothes. "Robert bought a lathe today. He's going to make soup bowls from the wood."

Robert is Mom's boyfriend. He's a bit of a jerk, but I can handle him.

"He could make you a spinning top too," I coo.

Leland scowls.

"The tree isn't happy," Mom says. "She's dying."

Leland's features soften. He takes a few sob-shuddered breaths. "Could I plant a seed from one of the apples?" he asks. "And grow another tree just like it?"

"Sure," Imogen says. "You could grow a tree exactly like it, if you want. But not from a seed. If you want a tree that's genetically the same as this one, you need to graft parts of this tree to the trunk of another apple tree."

"Graft?" Silas says. "You stick them together, right? And they grow into one tree."

"Black electrician's tape does the trick," Imogen says." But I've got to cut them just right, and it's got to be done in spring."

Leland sniffs and looks at Mom. "Can we?"

"That's a great idea," Mom smiles.

"I'll cut a few scions—those are small branches," Imogen explains. "We'll keep them somewhere dark and cool until grafting time."

"Under my bed?" Leland suggests.

Imogen laughs. "Let's bury them in your yard. In a plastic bag. The earth is nice and cool."

"We can mark the spot with rocks!" Silas cries.

"Like a gravestone," Leland says grimly.

"No," Silas says. "Like buried treasure!"

Imogen pulls a penknife from her pocket. "Okay, everyone?"

"I'll get some ziplock bags," Mom says.

After we bury the scions, Mom packs the boys off to the playground so they don't have to witness the destruction.

We picked the last apples a few days ago. Now we dismantle the tree house. We pry out nails and pull down board after board.

After that, Imogen fires up the chain saw. It whines and gripes, tearing up the afternoon air with its noise. It growls through branch after branch. The limbs crash to the ground and stay where they fall. I half-imagined they'd get up and walk away, as if freed. But no. This is the end.

Imogen chooses a few thick pieces for Robert to turn on his lathe. The rest she bucks into firewood, which I stack under the porch.

As we work, Imogen tells me she grew up in the North, in the forest. Her parents were "back-to-the-landers." They lived off the land as much as possible.

They hunted deer, gathered berries, raised sheep for wool. From the age of six, Imogen was chopping wood for the woodstove.

"Apple wood burns long and hotter than most woods. It smells supersweet," Imogen says dreamily as she pours tea from her thermos. "You guys will have a cozy winter."

She is perched on the stump of our old tree. The yard looks bald and exposed. The gentle drifts of sawdust belie the savagery.

"It's always sad to see an apple tree go," Imogen says. "The people of Vancouver Island used to grow most of their food. Now, we get food from a truck or barge or container ship. And you can bet it wasn't grown on a family farm. Chances are the food you eat traveled more than five hundred miles to get to your belly. It's crazy.

I got a blackberry Popsicle this summer that was made in Florida! It came from the opposite corner of the continent in a refrigerated truck!"

"That's a lot of gasoline," I said.

"You know what's in a blackberry Popsicle? Blackberries and water. Blackberries grow like weeds around here, and water—well, it falls on us half the year." Sure enough, a light rain had begun to fall.

"My neighbors grow food in their backyard," I say, thinking of Olive's family.

"Oh, yeah. People are starting to farm again—in the city too. The mayor recently planted tomatoes and kale at city hall. My friend Valerie gathers her own salt. She boils ocean water on the stove until the water steams off. She follows the 100-Mile Diet. She doesn't eat anything grown more than a hundred miles away. I'm working on a ten-*meter* diet. This past spring, my landlord let me put a vegetable garden in the back of the apartment building. I'd been guerrilla gardening back there for years anyway."

"Guerrilla gardening?" I ask.

"Yeah. I grew tomatoes and peas in an area behind the garage without him knowing. Guerrilla gardeners do this all over the world. They take over land that isn't being used—or that's being badly used—and grow food. Some grow wildflowers to add beauty to a derelict area. There's a group that drops seed bombs from airplanes. They make 'bombs' of dirt and compost crammed with wildflower seeds. On International Sunflower Guerilla Gardening Day, May 1, thousands of people around the world plant sunflower seeds in public places. Imagine: sunflowers sprout up in parking lots, outside of banks, along highways and bike paths.

"People have gardened like this for hundreds of years. There are apple trees along the banks of the canals in northern Utah that were planted one hundred and fifty years ago by the people who dug the canals. They buried apple cores from their lunches in the freshly turned soil, knowing they'd be back one day to collect the apples. In South Africa, the very poor who live in slums plant vegetables on any spare bit of land. It brings them together as a community."

"I'm doing a project on South Africa for school," I tell her.

"So you know about Nelson Mandela?"

"Yeah. Cool guy!" Mandela was South Africa's president from 1994 to 1999. When he was young, he fought against his country's racist government. He was put in jail. Mandela is black, as are most South Africans. The government enforced apartheid, which means "apartness."

Only white people could be in power. White people had tons of money and land. Everyone else got the toughest jobs, the worst land and the crummiest schools. Black girls weren't even allowed to go to school.

People all over the world fought against apartheid. Countries wouldn't trade with South Africa. Mom says that for years neither she nor any of her friends would buy anything made in South Africa. Finally apartheid ended, and Mandela was released from prison. Soon after that he was elected president.

"He was in jail for *twenty-seven years*," Imogen says, shaking her head.

"Yeah. He taught the other inmates about the law and human rights. The jail was known as 'Mandela University,'" I say.

"He also planted a garden on the prison roof so the inmates could have fresh vegetables," Imogen says.

I didn't know that.

"There was so much produce, the prison guards brought sacks for Mandela to fill. He actually grew food for his jailers! He said a garden was one of the few things in prison that a person could control: 'To plant a seed, watch it grow, to tend it and then harvest it, offered...a taste of freedom.' That's what guerrilla gardening is about: freedom, the freedom to choose what you eat and to work and feast with your neighbors. Food tastes better when it is grown on the land where you live."

"Yeah, I know," I say. I kick at the pile of boards on the ground. I am interested in what Imogen is saying, but now I am drenched with sadness. "We used to pick apples straight from the tree house. They were the best apples I ever ate."

Imogen gives me a sympathetic frown. Then she shrugs. "Cheer up!

It couldn't live forever. The oldest apple tree is one hundred and eighty-five years old. It's in Vancouver. They've got a fence around it and everything. Yours did very well. Listen, come and see my garden tomorrow. I just planted chard and broccoli—they can survive the winter. Bring your bike. I'll give you a tour of a few local guerrilla gardens."

Chapter Eleven

We pass Richard's bench on the way to school each day, but I don't look at it anymore. I'm still mad at Richard for making me feel bad. Or, I don't know, maybe for not being around when I have all these questions. Maybe I'm angry because I think my anger will wake him up—to defend himself.

Even though I don't look at Richard's bench, I still get a feeling that he's watching me when I walk through. One day, as we're walking to school, Silas says, "Stop. Let's tidy up."

Leland says, "Good idea."

The sunflower is shriveled up, and the seat of the bench is littered with curling yellow leaves. I wipe the photo frame clean with my sleeve. Leland clears the leaves from the bench.

The rain and sun have faded the Rest in Peace sign to a blank page. Silas gets a pen and paper from his backpack and makes a new one.

I gather a bouquet to lay on the bench. There aren't many flowers at this time of year, so I collect small evergreen branches from the ground. I search under the skirt of a cedar tree and am jolted by what I see.

At the base of the tree is an old wool blanket in a clump, a sleeping bag with fiberfill fizzing through its large holes and a dirty pillow. Beside the bedding are three blackened candle stubs, a couple of forks, a bent spoon, a can-opener and three unopened cans. There are Heinz Baked Beans, Alphagetti and Chef Boyardee Ravioli. They are what my mom calls "non-food."

It's damp under the tree, but it's protected. I look at the spiraling branches above and imagine the moonlight sifting down. It could be beautiful. But mostly, it feels primitive and cramped.

"Liza?" Silas sounds ready to go. I hurry out from under the boughs. I don't want him to see. I don't know if it was Richard's sleeping place, but I have a strong urge to protect the little bit of privacy Richard had.

At school we pass the planter where the boys and I had snacks before the funeral. Out of the corner of my eye, I notice green sprigs shooting out of the carrot tops we shoved into the dirt. They look triumphant. They give me a thrill.

Moments later Niall stops me outside class. He's shaking with anger. "She said it would be too smelly! No, she said 'too odorific,'" he seethes. "Can you believe it?"

Just then a clunk sounds through the PA system. Mrs. Reynolds's voice squeaks nasally. "I'd like to remind everyone to be careful of the flagpole in the front schoolyard. A flag is a very important symbol. So, please, keep your distance."

Niall and I laugh. Niall says he's going to give the petition to the vice-principal and send it to the head of the school board. I suggest he send it to the editor of the city's daily paper.

"Good idea." He nods. Then he slumps against the wall. "I've got to say, I'm getting tired of asking."

That afternoon I'm in class staring out the window at the schoolyard when

I notice that a swath of grass has been dug up. A huge patch of dirt has been laid bare. I look at the blank blackboard at the front of the room, then back at the patch of dirt. They have the same message: *Make a mark. Create. Invent.*

As the blackboard fills with math equations, I glance down at the rectangle of dirt and imagine it as a BMX track or a tennis court or a dance floor.

After school, I pass Mr. Moyle, our school custodian, turning the dirt with a shovel.

"The grass was getting choked out by a nasty weed that I couldn't fully uproot," he explains when I ask what's going on. "I had to dig the whole thing up. I'll be reseeding in a couple of weeks."

"With what?" I ask.

"Grass," he answers. "Of course."

I stare at the patch of dirt, imagining a carpet of grass. In my mind, the grass suffocates the dirt. Then I notice Mr. Moyle is giving me a quizzical look.

On my way home through the park, there's rustling again in the bushes near Richard's bench. I'm on my own. I feel frightened and excited. It's silly, but I call out, "Richard?" The bushes rustle again, but nothing emerges. I run home as fast as I can. I race straight to my room.

"Liza?" Mom is at my door. "Would you like a cup of tea?"

"No thanks," I say. I'm lying face-down on my bed.

"Are you okay?"

"Yeah."

"Can I come in?"

"Sure."

Mom sits on the edge of my bed. She hands me a cup of tea. I take a deep breath and ask, "Mom, do we even know that Richard's dead? I mean, those ashes in that box. No one saw them. They could have been Cheerios."

"Cheerios?" Mom laughs.

"Who saw his body, anyway? Who found Richard?"

"Richard is dead, Liza. There isn't any doubt." Mom rubs my back.

"You wouldn't know it by the way you and the boys act," I say peevishly.

"What do you mean?"

"I mean you guys act as if nothing's changed. You chat with your friends about the weather. On the morning he died, the boys played Lego!"

"Liza, Silas was crying so hard that day, I had to get him out of school early. But I don't have to prove how he feels. People mourn in different ways, but we all feel sad. We also feel angry and confused. Sometimes, we even deny that the person died. Honey, you can't judge what's inside someone's heart by how they act. You have to ask."

"Yeah, that's the problem. I wish I knew how Richard *felt* all those years."

"I do too. I wish I'd asked."

"Me too."

The world goes silent then. We both slurp our tea.

The next day Niall and I are talking in the hallway when Mr. Moyle shuffles by with his shovel. As I watch him head outside, my brain ignites with the best idea I've ever had. I tingle all over. I can almost hear my brain synapses snap and sizzle.

"Are you okay?" Niall asks, smiling.

"I'm fine," I say. I decide to keep my sizzling idea to myself for now.

Mom always says, "Let it percolate before you pour." For once I will take her advice.

I spend the next two days percolating. I gaze out the classroom window at that swath of dirt where anything could go. Plain, boring, inedible grass is an insult. It's like asking an opera singer to sing "Mary Had a Little Lamb" or a chef to cook Kraft Dinner. I remember the lines Mom read at the memorial: *Turn me into song; sing me awake*. I imagine plants bursting up from that brown pool. I see vines and branches rustling and pulsing with nourishment, their fruit swelling.

My idea is good.

"Mrs. Reynolds!" I burst into her office at lunch. Words tumble out of me. "The dirt in the side yard. Could GRRR! plant a garden there? Like Nelson Mandela did when he was in prison? Each class could take turns looking after it."

Mrs. Reynolds doesn't even consider it. "No," she says.

"But we'd have fresh food. Kids could learn how things grow."

"Students would track dirt into the school. It would look untidy. Strangers would take the food."

"So what? They'd be *eating* it."

"No."

"But—"

"No, Liza Maybird," she says. "And I don't appreciate your insinuation that this school is like a South African prison."

"It didn't used to be!"

"Get to class. Or I will see you in detention."

Now I understand Niall's fury.

When I go outside for recess, I wonder if seeing the patch of dirt will anger me more. Instead it slows me right down. It is simply "there," free of expectation. It's patient like Richard.

What had he missed out on? What had he dreamed of doing when he was my age?

Now, I imagine Richard happy and golden on his bench. I see sprigs of green reaching, small explosions of color. I know what I am going to do. I only hope the girls of GRRR! will get on board.

Chapter Twelve

Leland, in his prize bowler hat, is at the front door handing out tickets as the girls arrive. Silas organizes the clothes into piles and stacks the books on the dining-room table. I've arranged my bedroom as a change area. I set up Mom's full-length mirror in the living room.

I'm serving Moroccan-style mint tea. I stuff loads of mint from our yard into tall glasses, add a tablespoon of sugar, pour in boiling water and stir. Silas yells that everything's ready, and we head into the living room. I've strung Christmas lights for ambience and put out chairs. The floor is covered in clothes. Finally, there's a knock at the door. Olive thinks we're going for a bike ride. I open the door and stand there grinning.

"What?" she asks.

Then everyone yells, "Surprise!" Olive looks into the living room and screams.

After the shock wears off, she sets down her helmet and examines the piles. She chooses a pair of skinny jeans and a striped T-shirt—a complete outfit. Then she chooses a book, *Island of the Blue Dolphins.* It is based on a true story of a twelve-year-old girl who survives alone on a California island for eighteen years. She builds a house of whale bones and sealskins, and she hunts birds at night. She even makes a skirt out of cormorant feathers.

My heart lurches when Olive chooses it. I want to read it again. Later, when Lizzie tries on my old jeans, I get the same feeling. I realize it isn't about the *things*—I've read that book a hundred times and those jeans don't fit me—it's about saying goodbye.

Mom says that in giving, we get more. She doesn't mean more stuff or money. I've asked. She means we feel more goodness. I get it. I watch my friends light up over their new clothes and books, and I feel good. I get some great scores too, which helps. I choose jean overalls with just the right bagginess and a T-shirt silk-screened with the image of a dragonfly breathing out fire. On my second round I take a cool wool kilt with silver clasp pin and a fantastic pair of slightly scuffed Oxford shoes.

We didn't waste our afternoon in a mall! And we had tons of laughs, especially over a padded bra that each of us tried on—as earmuffs, knee protectors, bunny ears. As the party winds down, Melissa and Emma T. head outside to play. They quickly return, shocked and unhappy.

"What happened to your tree house?" Melissa asks.

"What happened to your *tree*?" Emma T. moans.

I tell everyone about honey fungus, and how the tree *had* to come down. They don't cheer up much. So I tell them about the scions that we'll graft onto a living tree in the spring. That helps, but they're still glum.

So I tell them my idea. I talk about "food miles" and the great taste of local food. And I tell them about the patch of dirt at school that's about to get "paved over" with grass.

"Why don't we go out one evening and plant it with food?" I say.

Three girls yell, "Yeah!" Everyone else is thoughtful.

"Wouldn't we get in huge trouble?" Afareen asks.

"For what? For planting food?" I ask.

"For going against the principal."

"The principal goes against us every step of the way," I say. "She doesn't care about the Earth. But we don't have time to *not* care. The ice caps are melting, and we're losing plant species every day. The time is now."

"We have to be able to look after it," Deirdre points out. "To water it and weed it."

"There's a water tap right there," I say. "My mom has an extra hose in the basement. We could schedule work parties."

"We could invite people to help," Deirdre muses. "Put up a sign, like,

If you eat this food, please give back by doing twenty minutes of weeding."

Everyone starts talking at once. Well, a few are quiet.

"No way," Olive finally says, shaking her head. "No way, no how. I'm not doing it."

"Come on, Olive," I urge. "We're making a point."

In the end, half of GRRR! likes the idea, a few are undecided and four, including Olive, are against it.

"If you do it, you can't claim it as a GRRR! action," Olive says. "We aren't all on board."

"Fine," I shout. I'm furious. I look out the window at the emptiness where the apple tree had been. I feel that a garden is owed to me. "Or maybe it means you aren't part of GRRR!"

The room goes silent. A few girls start gathering their clothes and books. When everyone is gone, I stomp to my room and give the lovers' telephone a yank. I mean to pull it out of Olive's window and back to my house, but it snaps in two.

That evening Olive and I don't talk. And we certainly don't meet in the tree house. I snap at Mom at supper and ask to be excused before dessert.

"You're tired," Mom says soothingly.

I'm tired, all right. I'm tired of Olive always being so careful and good. Also, I think furiously, I organized the clothing exchange for her, and she never thanked me.

Chapter Thirteen

"Nice outfit," Mom says at breakfast. I'm wearing my kilt with the dragonfly T-shirt and leg warmers I made last night. I used the sleeves of an old sweater. "I noticed Deirdre got the dress you practically lived in last summer," Mom says. "I'm surprised you gave it away."

"It was hard to give stuff up at first," I admit. "Even if it didn't fit me anymore. But it got easier. I mean, the dress doesn't mind who wears it."

"One of my favorite writers, George Bernard Shaw, said people become more attached to their burdens than their burdens are to them," Mom says.

"Cool," I say. I wonder if Olive is a burden. Maybe I'm more attached to her than she is to me.

"Hey, Liza?" Leland asks. "Did Silas and I do a good job helping with the clothing exchange?"

"Yes, of course you did."

"Oh."

"Why?"

"You never said thanks."

"I didn't?"

"No," Silas says.

"Sorry, you guys," I say. "Thank you.

Thank you very much. You were amazing."

I take ten deep breaths, reach for the phone and dial Niall's number. He's busy on the roof, his mom tells me. She asks if I could swing by. I hop on my bike and pedal through the park. I stop at Richard's bench for a moment, but I don't feel that he's watching anymore. It's just a little lonely.

Then there's a rustling in the bushes. A large raccoon wanders out, sniffing at the ground. It's not at all interested in me.

Niall's house is what you call ramshackle. It's an old shingled thing, painted light blue.

Three teenagers are doing surgery on an old car in the driveway. Two ancient-looking cats snooze on frayed rattan chairs on the rickety porch.

A mower sits in the middle of the overgrown lawn. Tumbledown as it is, it's alive. I'd take this place over a five-thousand-square-foot mansion anytime.

Niall's mom emerges with a pie in her hands and points upward. Niall is on the roof, wrestling with what looks like a black snake. "He's building us a solar shower." His mom beams. "Niall, you've got a visitor!"

"Niall's got a visitor!" the teenagers tease. My face gets hot. Niall looks down and smiles. "Come on up!"

His mom sends me up the ladder with a plate of pie and a mug of tea for us to share. It's an awkward climb.

As we sip tea, I tell Niall my idea and GRRR!'s plans. He immediately starts planning an irrigation system. "I'm glad you want to help," I interrupt. "I'm also hoping, well, that BRRR! will agree to us using the three hundred dollars from the bike wash. We could use it for plants and tools."

Niall looks at me funny. He studies my nose, lips, hair. He catches me watching him and gulps.

"Okay," he blurts. "I'll talk to the guys. I'll call you later—or how about I bike to your place?"

"Sure," I say, while my heart flops about like a fish in a net.

That evening Olive arrives at the back door with a coil of hose in her hands.

I break into a wide smile. "So you're going to help out after all!"

"No," Olive says firmly. "Liza, I'm sorry, but I don't *always* have to agree with you. And you know I'm a scaredy-cat."

"Yeah, I know that," I mutter. We both smile. "This is for the speaking tube you've been meaning to make. The tin can phone broke." She looks me in the eye. I know she knows I broke it. I also know she has been crying. "And I found these." She pulls out two funnels. All I have to do is tape the funnels to the hose, one at each end, and our speaking tube is done. Wealthy people used to use speaking tubes to talk to their driver from the backseat of the Rolls or with the servants in other parts of the house. Nowadays they're only seen on submarines and in playgrounds.

"I also want to thank you for the clothing and book exchange," Olive says. "It was really cool."

"Yeah," I say. "That's okay."

"And Liza?"

"Yeah?"

"Do you still have that padded bra?"

"What do you need it for?" I ask. But one look at her and I burst out laughing.

She has the funnels under her shirt. We laugh together. Then we get out the electrician's tape and work on our communication system.

Chapter Fourteen

I spend a few afternoons with Imogen. We cycle around town, meeting gardener friends of hers. There are some amazing secret gardens in the city. A group called Dogwood Initiative is taking over vacant lots to grow food for anyone to pick. A lot of people talk about seed sharing as a way to keep a variety of seeds in circulation to ensure biodiversity. A few give me baggies of seeds with names like Monster Kale or Bliss Garlic. Everyone says that their own food tastes best.

One of Imogen's friends talks about food security. That means that everyone should be able to access nutritious food. Everyone in the world should have enough money to buy food or land to grow their own. The food should also be appropriate to how people live. So if they're vegetarian, they should be able to get vegetarian food. Food security also means that the food is raised in a safe way—safe for the environment and for people's health.

One day Imogen leads a bicycle tour of GRRR! and BRRR! members to a "farm" in the city. It is a house where the yard has been completely turned into garden beds. We get lessons in mixing soil and planting swiftly and secretly.

A couple of nights later, we're ready. After dark, Melissa, Afareen, Hayiko,

Emma T., Niall and I bike through the quiet streets. We are pulling trailers of compost and plants and shovels. We use bungee cords to strap everything snugly so that nothing rattles.

Imogen found the plants for us. She also landed us a load of free horse manure. Free poo! And she checked the site to make sure the soil was well drained and had good sun exposure.

Niall and I drew up a schedule that breaks our mission into half minutes. We move quickly and quietly. After the planting is done, we spread wood shavings to keep the roots warm. Cars pass by, but no one slows down. We're done in forty minutes.

Half a block away we stop and consider our work. We've planted ten young apple trees. They look like humble umbrellas. It's a sweet orchard. We planted garlic, chives and leek around the trees as companion plants.

They will help the apple trees grow. Afareen painted a beautiful sign that reads:

Apples for All
A community orchard

A second sign explains that all are welcome to help care for and reap the rewards of this orchard, which will bear fruit in two years. It is signed *GRRR! and BRRR!*

I take Niall's hand and squeeze it. He squeezes back. Then we're back on our bikes, whooping for joy as we pedal down the dark roads. That night, a soft rain falls on the house. I imagine the trees lapping up the fresh water.

Chapter Fifteen

Ri-i-i-ing. Ri-i-i-ing. Ri-i-i-ing. Ri-i-i-ing. I lift my head from the pillow and think, *There is something new and wonderful in the world, stretching its branches.* Mom gets the phone. A second later, she's in my room.

"Liza! What have you done?"

"It's beautiful, Mom," I murmur sleepily. "It's for everyone."

"Mrs. Reynolds is calling it vandalism. She mentioned expulsion."

"Expulsion?"

"As in getting kicked out of school. For trespassing. Destruction of property."

"All we did was plant fruit trees. That dirt wasn't being used. It's not like we broke windows or set fire to a garbage can."

"Why didn't you get permission?"

I sat up. "We tried, Mom. Many times. Reynolds wouldn't even listen. She's been dying to expel someone since day one."

"Your fingernails are dirty." Mom moans as if I'm a criminal with blood on my hands. "Why didn't you tell me?"

"I wanted it to be a surprise. A sudden thing. Sudden beauty."

"What gave you the idea?"

I thought this over. "The earth did," I finally say. "That patch of dirt. And—Richard."

Mom's face crumples with sympathy. "Richard?" she whispers.

I tell her about the apple Leland left on Richard's bench. Then I talk about food banks and the non-food I found under the tree and how Richard tried to gather windfall. How apples are shipped from as far away as Mexico and Australia when we could grow all we need here. I talk about how kids who live near gardens are happier.

"But how did you? Where did you get the trees?"

"We just did," I mumble, shrugging.

"*Liza.*"

"Okay. Okay. Imogen. The money came from BRRR! From Niall." I get a thrill saying his name, and I feel in less trouble.

"I have to think about this, Liza. Mrs. Reynolds wants to meet with all the kids involved."

"When?"

"*Now.*"

Silas and Leland have been standing in my doorway listening. "Are you in trouble, Liza?" Leland asks.

"I guess so. For planting a garden. A small orchard."

"That sounds nice," says Silas.

"You should have asked, Liza," Mom scolds.

"I *did* ask. You're the one who always says, 'Don't take no for an answer.' You're the one who threw eggs at the Department of National Defence when Canada helped invade Iraq."

"That was a long time ago," Mom says.

"Well, I'm a long time ago!" I say.

Mom looks at me. "They do say the apple doesn't fall far from the tree."

"Unless there's a really big breeze?" Leland asks.

Silas and I laugh. Mom doesn't. She sends me a look that's like a blast of cold wind. *Then* she smiles.

When we reach school, our orchard is surrounded by parents as well as kids. A police officer is taking notes. She makes my heart lurch. Niall looks as confident as ever. He's even smiling. It feels good to have a partner in this.

"Wow," Leland breathes when he sees the orchard. "So that's sudden beauty."

Niall, Emma T., Afareen, Melissa and I, and a few parents file into Mrs. Reynolds's office. Her hands shake as she draws the blinds.

"I do all I can to run a tidy school," she rages. "I expect to be respected. But you! You vandals think you can trespass and destroy."

"It's a *public* school," I say. "Public means we have some say in how things are done. We asked for a composting program and for a solar hot-water system on the roof and for this garden. We asked for some way to do something green. You don't even hear us. You just say, 'Get to class.' This isn't about destruction. It's about the amazing taste of an apple grown in your own neighborhood."

"Students could learn about pollination and photosynthesis with this garden," Niall argues. "About soil and seeds."

"They'd learn that food comes from plants, not packages," I add.

"I have called in a bulldozer," says Mrs. Reynolds.

"You will destroy the plants," Mom muses, "and then plant grass?"

"We will remove the trees," Mrs. Reynolds says. "I am talking with the district supervisor about what to do with you lot."

Melissa starts crying. Hayiko nervously runs the zipper of her hoodie up and down. I glance at our vice-principal, who is normally nice. I raise my eyebrows to encourage him to offer some perspective. He clears his throat and says nothing.

There is a quick knock on the door, and Mr. Moyle hurries in, talking. "I didn't know you were putting in fruit trees," he says to Mrs. Reynolds. "Great idea! They look fantastic!"

Niall elbows me. A couple of the kids giggle. Mrs. Reynolds gives a sickly smile. On his way out, Mr. Moyle gives me the quickest of winks.

"Everyone out," Mrs. Reynolds barks. "We'll meet here at recess."

But we never have that second meeting. Recess is a five-ring circus. Silas spent the morning in the bathroom making protest signs. Then he got all his buddies to "defend the trees." A hundred kids are circling the orchard chanting, "We love apples."

At one point, Mme. Falette gives me a quiet thumbs-up. Pretty soon, news cameras arrive.

We lift the TV onto the end of the dining table so we can watch while we eat supper. There I am, standing in the schoolyard, looking into the camera: Liza Maybird, "Guerilla Gardener." I say that what we did was harmless and was meant to raise awareness as much as to grow apples.

Mrs. Reynolds appears sharp and humorless.

In our kitchen Silas and Leland boo when she appears on the screen, but Mom tells them to be respectful.

Reporters ask Mrs. Reynolds if she'll let the children keep the orchard. She says "no." Then her cell phone rings.

On camera! "Excuse me," she says sourly. A moment later she turns off her phone. "That was the school board," she says through clenched teeth. "If the students can look after it, the orchard can stay."

We whoop and holler. "Shhh," Mom says.

On the television, Mrs. Reynolds is still talking. "You can bet the kids who did this will be doing the bulk of the weeding and watering and pruning. That will be their punishment!"

After supper, I chat online with my old friend Jamaica, an activist in the United States who keeps tabs on the oil industry. She says that what we did was called proactive activism and civil disobedience. *Civil disobedience is when people—usually peacefully—disobey a law or a government's command because they see it as unfair*, she writes. *Proactive activism is when you do something toward a more sustainable, just world. Rather than just complain, you build something good. Way to go, Liza!*

Niall and I talk on the phone for thirty-eight minutes.

"Were you ever scared?" I ask.

"I was only scared that you might back out and leave me holding the watering can!" he said. "Were *you* ever scared, Liza?"

"Yes," I admit. "I was scared when Richard died. He left a hole. I was afraid we'd all fall through."

After I hang up, Silas says. "I heard what you said about Richard. It's true. He was a like a knot that held our neighborhood together."

"The plug that keeps the water in the sink," Leland adds. A while later he taps me on the shoulder. He has made a sign that says *Richard's Orchard*. His letters are kind of messy, but they look alive.

Olive reports through the speaking tube that her family is making a bench for the orchard out of shipping pallets they scavenged.

"My parents want to help, even if they aren't sure they agree with what you did," Olive says.

"I'm not sure *I* agree with what we did," I confess. "But I'm glad we did it."

It's spring again. Imogen, Mom, Leland and I watch as Silas sweeps aside the grass and locates the circle of stones we left as a marker. Imogen digs up the scions, then binds three of them to three root stocks. We've decided we can fit three apple trees in the backyard. They'll have each other for company.

"How soon before the scion and root stock become one tree?" I ask.

"As soon as their sap meets," Imogen answers.

The trees won't produce apples this year, and probably not next year either. But the following year, it will. And for many years afterward.

"These trees could be producing apples long after we're all laid in the ground," Imogen says, standing back to survey her work.

"Good," I say. I think of Richard. I take in the whole moment—the air, the earth, my brothers, Mom, Imogen, even myself. "Good," I say again.

Sara Cassidy has worked as a professional clown, a youth-hostel manager, a tree planter in five Canadian provinces, and as a human-rights witness in Guatemala. Her poetry, fiction and articles have been widely published. *Windfall* is Sara's second entry in the Orca Currents series. Her first Current, *Slick*, also features Liza and the girls of GRRR!

orca *currents*

978-1-55469-352-8 $9.95 pb
978-1-55469-353-5 $16.95 lib

Liza is determined to prove that her mother's boyfriend is no good. When she discovers that the oil company Robert works for has come under criticism for its actions in Guatemala, she's certain she's struck gold—or rather, oil. Liza decides to expose Robert's evil ways by exposing his company's actions. She puts together a girls' group called GRRR!—Girls for Renewable Resources, Really!—and learns just how much power can be generated by a pack of girls.

orca currents

978-1-55469-816-5 $9.95 pb
978-1-55469-817-2 $16.95 lib

Since the death of his father, everyone has been telling Cam that he's the man of the house. Cam takes his responsibility seriously. He keeps the grieving household organized and takes care of his sister. But when the man who had been driving the truck that killed his father seems to be stalking his family, he is not sure he's up for the task. How does the man of the house handle a stalker?

Titles in the Series

orca *currents*

121 Express
Monique Polak

Bear Market
Michele Martin Bossley

Benched
Cristy Watson

Beyond Repair
Lois Peterson

The Big Dip
Melanie Jackson

Bio-pirate
Michele Martin Bossley

Blob
Frieda Wishinsky

Branded
Eric Walters

Camp Wild
Pam Withers

Chat Room
Kristin Butcher

Cheat
Kristin Butcher

Cracked
Michele Martin Bossley

Crossbow
Dayle Campbell Gaetz

Daredevil Club
Pam Withers

Dog Walker
Karen Spafford-Fitz

Explore
Christy Goerzen

Fast Slide
Melanie Jackson

Finding Elmo
Monique Polak

Flower Power
Anne Walsh

Fraud Squad
Michele Martin Bossley

Horse Power
Anne Walsh

Hypnotized
Don Trembath

In a Flash
Eric Walters

Junkyard Dog
Monique Polak

Laggan Lard Butts
Eric Walters

Manga Touch
Jacqueline Pearce

Marked
Norah McClintock

Mirror Image
K.L. Denman

Nine Doors
Vicki Grant

Perfect Revenge
K.L. Denman

Pigboy
Vicki Grant

Queen of the Toilet Bowl
Frieda Wishinsky

Rebel's Tag
K.L. Denman

Reckless
Lesley Choyce

See No Evil
Diane Young

Sewer Rats
Sigmund Brouwer

The Shade
K.L. Denman

Skate Freak
Lesley Choyce

Slick
Sara Cassidy

The Snowball Effect
Deb Loughead

Special Edward
Eric Walters

Splat!
Eric Walters

Spoiled Rotten
Dayle Campbell Gaetz

Storm Tide
Kari Jones

Struck
Deb Loughead

Sudden Impact
Lesley Choyce

Swiped
Michele Martin Bossley

Watch Me
Norah McClintock

Windfall
Sara Cassidy

Wired
Sigmund Brouwer

orca *currents*

For more information on all the books in the Orca Currents series, please visit **www.orcabook.com.**